The

Beat the Bullies

Michele Elliott is the Director of Kidscape, set up after a very successful pilot study involving thousands of parents, teachers and children being taught 'good sense defence'. A teacher, child education psychologist and mother of two, she has worked with children and adults for twenty-two years.

She is on the advisory councils of the NSPCC and ChildLine and has been awarded a Winston Churchill Fellowship.

Also by Michele Elliott

The Willow Street Kids: Be Smart, Stay Safe

The Willow Street Kids

Beat the Bullies

Michele Elliott

MACMILLAN CHILDREN'S BOOKS

First published 1993 as *The Bullies Meet The Willow Street Kids*
by Pan Macmillan Children's Books

This edition published 1997 by Macmillan Children's Books
a division of Macmillan Publishers Ltd
25 Eccleston Place, London SW1W 9NF
and Basingstoke

Associated companies throughout the world

ISBN 0 330 35185 0

1 3 5 7 9 8 6 4 2

A CIP catalogue record for this book is available from
the British Library

Phototypeset by Intype London Ltd
Printed by Mackays of Chatham plc, Chatham, Kent

Contents

Foreword   vii
1 The Bully is Back   1
2 Charlie is Hurt   9
3 Willow Street Kids Reunited   15
4 Lunchtime Surprise   19
5 Marilyn's Terror   27
6 Guess   33
7 The Bullies Come Back   41
8 What To Do   47
9 Telling   55
10 Marilyn Makes Friends   63
11 Justice   69
12 Snowed In – Hurray!   77
Epilogue   83

Appendix   85
  Help!   85
  Resources   85

For Katharine Bamber,
in the hope that we can stop bullying
for children everywhere.

Foreword

Dear Reader,

Bullying is a problem that affects us all. The bully is an unhappy, cowardly person. Those who are being bullied are also unhappy, through no fault of their own. In *The Bullies Meet The Willow Street Kids*, Gill and Charlie and their friends meet and deal with bullies, with the help of teachers and parents.

No one deserves to be bullied. Perhaps by reading this book you will get some ideas about what to do, in case it happens to you.

The most important thing to remember is that, if you are being bullied, tell someone. Don't keep it to yourself. Tell your parents, a teacher, a friend or ring one of the organizations, such as ChildLine, listed at the back of this book. And keep telling until someone listens and helps you.

Our charity for children, Kidscape, can send you a free twenty-page booklet to give you more ideas. Write to:

> Kidscape
> 152 Buckingham Palace Road
> London SW1W 9TR

and ask for the *Stop Bullying!* booklet. Be sure to include your name and address.

Many of you have read the first book in this series, *The Willow Street Kids*, and written to ask for a second book. Here it is – I hope you enjoy it!

Michele Elliott

CHAPTER ONE

The Bully is Back

Gill could hardly believe her eyes. There she was, larger than life – the girl who had bullied them . . . who had taken Katie's money a couple of summers ago in this same corner of the park. What was she doing? Gill remembered exactly what had happened. She and the rest of her friends had arranged to meet in the park on the last day of the summer holidays. It was going to be the final chance to mess around before going back to homework and tests and all that. The weather was great, and the food . . . Gill sighed. She did so love food.

Katie had gone to ring her mother. The bully had surprised her and stolen her money. But Gill and her friends had managed to get it back. Gill smiled when she thought about their triumph; she almost forgot about watching the bully.

Just then the girl looked around, sending Gill racing behind a tree. Her heart felt like a jumping ping-pong ball. *Hope she doesn't see me*, thought Gill. *She looks like she's up to no good.*

'Hi, Gill!' shouted Charlie, coming up behind her. 'What on earth are you doing?'

Gill shrieked and jumped ten metres into the air. 'Shhh! You loud-mouth turkey! Can't you see who's over there?' Gill motioned Charlie to her. Charlie peered around the tree.

'Who's she, anyway?'

'What do you mean?' hissed Gill. 'That's the girl who took Katie's money. You remember. She's the one with the spiky hair – the one we caught!'

Charlie looked puzzled. He screwed up his face until his freckles almost merged. He looked rather like a pizza when he did that, thought Gill. Then the light dawned. 'Oh, I remember. We caught up with her and surrounded her on our bikes. She wasn't so brave then. I got Katie's money back.'

'Don't you mean *we* got Katie's money back?'

Charlie shrugged.

'Anyway, Sherlock, remind me not to ask you for clues on the next murder case. Your memory is seriously flawed. Detectives have to remember all the details.'

'What murder case?'

'Never mind – it was just a joke!' Gill despaired. Charlie could be so exasperating.

Charlie grinned, his freckles leaping apart. There was nothing he liked better than winding up his friends, particularly Gill. With her ginger hair and green eyes, she always reminded him of a cat. A cat with claws. He ducked as she poked at him.

'Missed. Anyway,' said Charlie, 'she looks different.'

'So do you after two years.' Gill looked around the tree again and let out another shriek, but this time it was dismay.

'What's the matter now?'

'She's gone. I wanted to follow her to see what she's up to. No good, if I'm right.'

'Forget her – let's go over to Tim's. I hear he's got a new computer game.'

'Yuck,' replied Gill. 'All you ever think of these days is how to get to the treasure without being eaten by the dragon or killed by a zillion warriors. Boring, I say. Fries your brain.'

'Fried Brain to Ginger. Come in, Ginger.'

Gill thought murder sounded like a good idea – perhaps with Charlie as the victim.

'See you later, then.' Charlie started to leave.

'Thanks a lot. First you scare me out of nine lives, then you go off to see if you can wipe out the bad guy on a computer.' Gill's voice was dripping with sarcasm. 'And, on top of it all, you make me lose sight of that bully.'

'What do you care, anyway? After all this time, it doesn't matter. Besides, we haven't seen Tim all summer. Much more fun than tailing a stupid bully.'

'Wait, there she is!' Gill shrank back and hid as best she could. The problem was that Gill was not little. In fact, she was decidedly plump, something that really bothered her, but she couldn't seem to do anything about it.

'Look, she's got other kids with her. I knew she was up to something.'

'Don't be daft, they aren't doing anything – just talking.'

'Go on then, go,' hissed Gill. 'Leave this to me.'

'Not on your life. If you stay, I stay.' Charlie wasn't so much loyal as curious. He didn't want to miss out on any excitement. Had he known what was going to happen, he might have changed his mind and played computer games instead.

They peered out from behind the tree for what seemed like ages. Nothing happened.

Patience was not one of Charlie's virtues. 'Come on, Gill, let's get out of here,' he whispered.

Gill ignored him. She had long ago decided that Charlie had the attention span of a gnat. Gill, of course, was made of sterner stuff. But even she was becoming a little restless. Being on stake-out seemed to have its dull moments. Television shows weren't like this.

At precisely that second, things started to move.

Two little kids came up the path towards the gang. They looked a bit apprehensive. In a flash, the gang grabbed them and pulled them into the bushes. It happened so quickly that Gill and Charlie could scarcely believe it.

There were muted screams and a brief struggle, with branches flying in all directions. Gill and Charlie raced towards them, but the gang had disappeared by the time they got there. It was all over in thirty seconds. As they reached the site of the crime, the two boys came out. The older had blood on his face, the younger a torn shirt. Both were shaking.

'You OK?' asked Charlie, wiping the blood off the older one's face.

The younger boy began to cry. 'They took our money. We're in big trouble when we get home. Dad said if it happened again, it was our fault for not fighting back.'

4

'Fighting back!' exclaimed Gill. 'Those kids are twice your size. I wouldn't fight them on a bet.'

'Try telling that to our dad,' said the older boy. 'Last time we got mugged, he nearly killed us for being sissies.'

'That's dumb,' muttered Charlie. 'Fighting them won't help – there's too many of them. Better to give up your money than get hurt.'

The boys didn't look convinced. The younger one clung to his brother, clasping his hand tightly.

'How many times have they done this to you?' Gill was beginning to see red. The bully had promised them she wouldn't do it again. So much for trusting bullies.

'Just a couple – we've got to go.' The older boy put his arm protectively around his brother, who was now sobbing even louder. He sounded like an elephant calling in the wild – although an elephant was probably quieter.

Gill and Charlie had to shout to be heard above the din. It was plain that Gill had detective blood. She fired questions at the brothers: 'Who are they?' 'Where do they jump you?' 'Could you identify them?' 'What're your names?'

The boys couldn't keep up. The older boy, Jamie, looked at Gill in astonishment.

'Er, what's all this got to do with you, anyway?'

Gill explained about the bully stealing Katie's money.

Charlie turned to Gill. 'Guess she didn't stop bullying just because we caught her. All that stuff about being afraid of a beating and pleading with us not to tell—'

'Yes,' Gill interrupted, 'and promising never to do it again. Hah! She's probably been bullying kids ever since we caught her.'

'She's a punky git!' exclaimed David, who had now stopped crying.

'I hate them all,' hissed Jamie.

'What do you want to do now?' asked Gill.

'I think we should call the police,' suggested Charlie.

'Good idea.'

'No way!' protested the boys. 'Our dad would kill us.'

They started running down the path, deaf to Gill and Charlie's entreaties. 'Come back!' they shouted together. 'Let's talk about it,' pleaded Gill.

But it was all to no avail. The boys had disappeared.

Gill and Charlie sat for a minute.

'Not fair, is it?' remarked Gill, sadly.

'Course not,' replied Charlie, 'but it's really nothing to do with us.'

'It is!' answered Gill emphatically. 'We had the same thing happen and that bully's getting away with it. Only she's getting meaner – she didn't hit us.'

'I'll bet that's because she didn't have her gang around. Big bully when she's got the power, big coward when she's caught alone. Makes me sick.'

Gill agreed. 'They didn't have to beat those kids – look at how little they were. I think we should go home and tell what happened.'

'Suits me,' replied Charlie. 'But I still want to go over to Tim's. Only a few days left until school starts and then we'll have too much homework to play games.'

'I wonder what it will be like at the big school,' mused Gill, as they got up and began to walk towards the gate.

'I'm not sure,' said Charlie. The thought of starting secondary school was exciting, but a bit worrying.

'There'll be a lot of kids we don't know,' said Gill.

Charlie nodded.

Neither of them saw the gang until it was too late.

CHAPTER TWO

Charlie is Hurt

'What have we here, Liz?' sneered a boy with long, dirty, stringy hair and several earrings in one ear.

'A couple of creeps, I reckon,' replied Liz. 'Why don't you teach them some manners, Brian?'

Brian grinned and bowed to Liz. The gang laughed. Then he reached over and pushed Charlie against the fence.

'Think you're a big man, do you? Guess you're not as big as you think, huh?'

Great, thought Gill. *We're in for it now.*

Charlie turned beetroot. His freckles pulsated on his face and his ears burned. He wanted to punch Brian right on the nose. He clenched his fists.

Brian turned to another boy. 'Would you look at that? Little spotted dick here thinks he's going to hit me. Come on, then, low-life – punch me.'

Charlie should have known better. Or at least listened to his own advice to Jamie and David, given just moments ago. But he was furious now, and when Charlie got furious he lashed out. Without a second thought, he ran at Brian, fists flailing. Brian put out his hand and held Charlie's head at arm's length. Charlie was swinging and yelling, but he couldn't land a blow on Brian. That made him even madder.

'Stop,' hissed Gill. 'There are six of them. It's no use.'

Charlie was so angry, he didn't hear Gill. He gave one last effort and broke free of Brian's grip. Then lunged into him, managing to land two blows before the whole gang was on him, punching, kicking and yelling obscenities.

Gill was horrified. She rushed towards Charlie, only to be flung back with one sweep of Liz's arm: 'Stay out of it, unless you want the same.'

Liz held Gill's arm behind her back and forced her to watch, absolutely helpless.

'Stop it, please!' Gill pleaded. 'They'll really hurt him.' Gill could feel her eyes filling with tears, but she willed them back. Crying would only make it worse, she reasoned.

'Listen, you little piece of . . .' Gill winced at the words. 'You asked for this and don't forget it.'

Charlie was moaning. Gill couldn't stand it any more.

'I'll do anything – just call them off!'

Liz grinned. 'Enough!' she shouted.

The gang stopped instantly and walked towards them. Gill could see Charlie lying on the ground. He looked awful.

'Right,' said Liz. 'Hand over all your money.' Gill did as she was told. The gang had already emptied out Charlie's pockets. Liz continued to hold Gill's arm behind her back. She could feel the blood throbbing near her elbow. Her hand was numb.

'Now, Red, the deal is this. You meet us here tomorrow, same time, same place, with more money.

You tell anyone and you're dead meat. We can find where you live, so don't try to be clever, or we'll get you alone and you won't like what we do.'

Liz wrenched Gill's arm higher up her back. Gill yelped with pain.

'Understand, dork?' Brian's face was centimetres from hers. Gill was terrified.

'Sure,' she managed to say between clenched teeth.

'I couldn't hear that, could you?' Liz turned to the rest of her gang.

'Sounded like a rat squealing to me,' said one.

'Or maybe a pig.'

They laughed uproariously.

Gill thought they were dumb, but she was in too much pain to do anything about it.

'I think she should get down on her knees and beg us.'

'Great idea, Al.'

Al looked pleased with himself.

Liz nearly pulled Gill's arm out of the socket, as she forced her to kneel.

'Beg us to forgive you for interfering with our work.' Brian was clearly enjoying this. The rest of the gang chorused their approval.

Gill felt humiliated . . . and angry. *I'll get you*, she thought. *Someday, you'll be sorry.*

Charlie moaned again. One of the gang started towards him.

'Wait!' gasped Gill. She had to do something to protect Charlie. She thought fast. Maybe a little false humility would work. Taking a deep breath, she said,

'I'm sorry we bothered you.' She tried her best to look humble, though she was seething inside. *Better to pretend than to have Charlie beaten to a pulp*, she thought.

'Say: "I'm sorry that I even live on the same planet with people as wonderful as you." ' Another girl, whom Liz called Digger, joined in the fun.

Gill repeated what she was told. She had no choice – there were six of them and Charlie was hurt. She had to get them to leave. Off in the distance, Gill could hear people approaching. *Let them see us*, she thought. *Please let them see us!*

Liz heard them, too. 'Come on,' she urged. 'Let's get out of here.' Giving Gill's arm one last pull, she shoved her so that Gill went sprawling on to the ground. 'Remember, meet us here tomorrow with money or we'll give you worse than this.'

Gill nodded, miserably.

Then the whole gang disappeared. *They're good at that*, thought Gill. She rushed over to Charlie. 'Are you all right?'

He looked up at her. He had a cut on his forehead and a bruise starting on his arm. 'Never felt better,' he said sarcastically.

Gill breathed a little easier. If Charlie was sarcastic, then he was going to be all right.

'You know,' said Charlie, 'I should've ignored them.'

'No kidding, Sherlock!'

Charlie stood up and gingerly touched his face. 'Nothing broken.'

'We'd better get you home,' Gill said, ushering

him towards the gate. 'And call the police. It isn't only bullying – it's *stealing*.'

'OK.' Charlie was in no shape to protest. 'Funny thing, back there . . .' he said, after a minute.

'Yeah – hysterical,' answered Gill.

'No, I mean that a couple of them were really hitting me. The rest seemed to be holding back. That's why I'm not hurt worse.'

'I wonder why?' mused Gill.

'Maybe some of them are just as scared of Liz as we are. Better to pretend to do what she says than to get bullied by her.'

'Could be, Sherlock. Maybe you have something there. The other strange thing is that she didn't recognize us.'

'If Katie had been here, or all of us together, she might have,' said Charlie, rubbing his head.

'Maybe,' answered Gill. 'Anyway, I'd love to get her – the great punky git!' She thought the brothers' description had been pretty accurate.

Charlie winced as he touched his wound. Now that it was over, he was fuming. 'How dare they attack us. We didn't do *anything* to them.' He strode on, getting angrier as he thought about it. His head hurt.

'Hey, wait!' shouted Gill.

Charlie hardly heard. 'They'll be sorry one day,' he vowed.

CHAPTER THREE

Willow Street Kids Reunited

Going to the new school was both exciting and scary. Gill and Deirdre walked along together, clutching their new school bags. Their mothers had offered to come, but neither girl wanted to look like a baby.

'I wish my mum was here,' whispered Deirdre, hoping none of the big kids would hear.

Gill nodded. 'Me too,' she replied. They had both heard stories about how the older kids at school picked on the younger ones. Just then she felt someone give her a push. Heart pounding, she turned, to see Charlie and Steve looking quite pleased with themselves.

'Didn't even hear us coming, did you, Sherlock!' Charlie had been waiting to get even with Gill for her remark. Joking about it helped Charlie – he was still furious and hurt by what had happened in the park.

'What *are* you talking about?' demanded Steve. 'Who's Sherlock?'

'Holmes, my dear Watson!' they replied in unison.

'No foolin'!' said Steve impatiently. 'I mean what do you mean?'

'What do you mean, what do I mean?' Gill loved to tease.

Steve rolled his eyes and sighed. 'Girls,' he said, silently swearing himself to everlasting bachelorhood.

Charlie winced and explained about the gang of bullies.

'You mean the same girl from a couple of years ago!' exclaimed Steve.

'The very same,' said Deirdre. Gill had told her all about it.

'Did you meet them the next day?'

'No way, José,' laughed Charlie.

'Well, don't keep me in suspense—' began Steve. He was cut off in mid-sentence by the arrival of the rest of their friends – Tim, Mark, Katie, Amy and Julia. They talked and howled and shrieked and yelled. No one heard anything anyone else said, but it didn't matter – they were together again after the holidays.

Tim had grown taller than Steve, but no one noticed, which Tim was delighted about. All summer he'd been with his relatives and every single one of them had said, 'My, haven't you grown?' or 'Getting to be quite the big boy, aren't we?' as they pinched his cheek, treating him like a three-year-old. It drove him berserk. Finally, he had said to one well-meaning uncle, 'That's my job – kids grow. Grown-ups notice – that's your job.' It was a take-off from a film he'd seen and he was being sarcastic. The trouble was that everyone had thought he was *so* cute. They'd repeated his comment with glee. Tim decided that when he was an adult, he would never ever say to a kid, 'My, how you've grown!' Being tall with glasses wasn't great anyway – he thought he looked like a 'brain'. Tim secretly wished he were more like Mark, who was athletic and strong.

'Hey,' said Steve, 'are you going to tell me the rest of the story?'

'What story?' shouted everyone.

So Gill and Charlie told it all over again.

'What happened?' demanded Amy. 'Did you catch them?'

'No,' said Charlie, embarrassed now by all the fuss. 'The police came and took details, but the bullies haven't shown up in the park again, so the police can't do anything.'

'What about the two boys?'

'Al and Brian? Never saw them again, either.'

'They probably guessed you'd tell.'

'No one would be silly enough to go back.'

'Don't be so sure,' commented Gill. 'Remember those brothers – they were giving the gang money all the time.'

'If I thought they would find out where I lived and come to my house,' said Charlie, 'I might have gone back just to keep them happy, especially if I had been on my own or younger.'

'When did this happen?' asked Julia.

'A few days ago,' replied Gill.

'See the scar over my eye?' Charlie became the object of great scrutiny.

'Wasn't the girl's name Judy?' said Katie. 'I'll never forget how scared I was when she took my money. But I am sure her name wasn't Liz.'

'That's right!' exclaimed Mark. 'I remember she told us her name – Judy.'

'Guess she's a liar, bully and a thief,' said Amy.

'I've got an idea,' said Katie. 'Let's go to the park after school and see if we can find them.'

'*Yes*!' everyone shouted. 'Let's do it!'

'I don't know,' Gill replied thoughtfully. 'My mum's forbidden me to go there until they're caught.'

'Me too,' said Charlie.

'Besides,' continued Gill, 'they're really mean. Big-time mean.'

'Then who's going to catch them? They can't be allowed to get away with this.' Steve was indignant. How dare they attack his friends!

Engrossed in their discussion, they suddenly realized that they had reached the school gates. They had to stop talking or else be late for the first day of classes.

'Well, good luck, everyone!'

'Yeah, see you at lunch.'

'Hope so.'

'Bye.'

'Bye.'

They had all been so busy talking that they failed to see a big girl with short, spiky hair, talking with her group of friends. But later they would be forced to notice the older group, with disastrous consequences.

CHAPTER FOUR

Lunchtime Surprise

Charlie looked around, unsure about what to do next. There didn't seem to be anyone in the room that he knew. People were laughing, jostling, getting trays full of food and sitting at tables.

Where's Mark? he thought. *He promised to meet me here at 12.15.* It was now 12.25 and no sign of him, or anyone else for that matter.

Charlie felt intimidated by all the noise and the size of the room. It was huge compared with his other school. He wished he was back there now, safe and secure with teachers and kids he knew. Maybe this growing up stuff wasn't so great. At least he had been the oldest last year, now he was the youngest again and he didn't like it one bit.

'Over here, Charlie!' called an unfamiliar voice. Relief swept over him – someone recognized him. He started in the direction of the voice and was nearly pushed over by a crowd of older kids.

'Watch where you're going, dweeb,' said one of them.

'Hi, Charlie,' he heard again. When he looked up, the crowd had landed at the table with the voice. He felt a twinge of disappointment. The boy who called him a dweeb was obviously called Charlie, as well. He

19

wondered how many more there were called Charlie. *Probably fifty*, he thought gloomily. *I'll change my name to Charlemagne*, he decided. *Bet there aren't many of them around. Or maybe Carl.* That exhausted his store of foreign language translations. He was so busy thinking up other unusual names that he didn't see Steve, Tim and Mark come up behind him.

'Hey!' yelled Steve. 'You awake?' Charlie jumped. They laughed.

'What's with you, man?' said Mark. 'You were supposed to meet us at the front of the canteen.'

'This *is* the front,' said Charlie, defensively.

'Uh, uh – no it's not. Look.' Tim was pointing to the sign clearly marked ENTRANCE.

'Well, what do you call that?' replied Charlie, pointing to another sign over the door he was standing by. It too said ENTRANCE.

'Truce.'

They got their trays and waited. 'Ugh! What a nasty smell!' Steve wrinkled his nose.

'Smells good to me,' said Mark.

'Well, you never had any sense. If it tastes as bad as it smells, I'm bringing my own lunch. My sister likes the food and that's reason enough for me *not* to.' Steve was certain. Anything his older sister liked, he knew had to be bad, *really* bad. Terri was only two years older, but treated him like a baby. Drove him up the wall. Well, things would be different now that they were in the same school. He was just as grown up as she was. At least she couldn't 'babysit' for him any more – he was too old for that, thank you very much!

'Well, some of us have already got more sense

than to eat this stuff.' Tim held up his lunch bag. 'I'll find a table.'

'Me, too,' said Julia. Amy and Mark also had their lunches, so they followed Tim.

Charlie, Gill, Steve, Deirdre and Katie stood talking in the queue. Deidre and Katie were complaining that they'd already been assigned homework in Maths.

'That's what you get for being smart,' said Gill. 'Should be in the lower Maths class like me – you know, the sort of two plus two equals five set. Our teacher didn't give us any homework because we're so hopeless.'

'Do you think we'll all be together in *any* class?' sighed Deirdre.

'So far, no luck, but what've you got after lunch?' They checked their schedules. Personal and Social Education was down for all of them, at the same time.

'Great!' said Deirdre. 'Let's see if the others are in the class, too.'

Going through the lunch line took ages. Steve and Charlie had hamburgers and chips with so much ketchup you couldn't see what they were eating. Deirdre had macaroni with cheese, a salad and a drink. Katie, who could eat and eat and *never* gain weight had so much food on her tray that Gill thought it would all slide off when she lifted it. It almost did, too. Gill chose a salad, an apple and a cup of soup. She was determined to keep her weight down, but it was so hard. How she envied Katie. They paid and carefully made their way back to the table where Tim and Amy were madly waving their arms in the air to attract their attention. The canteen looked like an airport departure lounge – so much space and so many tables. Sounded like a runway at take-off, as well: they could hardly hear themselves talk.

'What took you so long?' asked Julia.

'Just about a million people trying to get served at the same time,' replied Steve. 'I'm definitely bringing my lunch from now.'

'Good idea,' said Gill. 'Look, you didn't even wait for us.'

'Didn't want our lunches to get cold,' replied Tim, grinning.

They talked about the summer, where they'd been, what they'd done, who they'd seen, but mostly about how big this new school was.

'Think I'll change my name,' commented Charlie to no one in particular.

'How about Joyce?' laughed Tim.

'Or Mildred?'

'Mary Lu?'

'Geraldine?'

'Very funny,' said Charlie. 'I'm serious – see that boy over there?' He pointed to the table where the other Charlie sat. He covered his finger with his other hand, just in case they looked up.

'His name is Charlie and there are probably a hundred more.'

'Sure,' smirked Tim, 'there must be at least a hundred, maybe two hundred.'

'Yup,' agreed Mark. 'There are one thousand kids in this school, so probably four hundred are called Charlie.'

Charlie turned away, sulking.

'Come on, don't be a dork. We're only teasing.'

Charlie was not amused.

They continued to eat and joke around. It was comforting to be together in this cavernous place. They all felt a bit lost and glad of the friendship that gave them someone to sit with. They finished their food, returned the trays and threw away their lunch bags.

'So, what do you think so far?' said Katie.

'OK,' said Gill. 'Except I don't like the gym teacher much.'

'You mean Ms Ogle. She's all right. She's just got a weird sense of humour, that's all.' Deirdre liked her.

'Yeah,' agreed Julia, 'don't take her too seriously.'

Gill wasn't convinced, but then she hated PE and having to undress for showers with all those girls she didn't know. Why couldn't they have privacy? *Bet the adults don't have to take showers together*, she thought.

'Hey, is everyone in Personal and Social Ed next?' asked Deirdre.

They found they were and all started talking at once. Steve held up his hand and shouted for attention. 'Anyone know the name of the teacher?' He smiled to himself. He knew something from his sister.

'No, what's her name?'

'His,' corrected Steve. 'Guess.'

'Smith?'

'Jones?'

'Charlie?'

Everyone had an idea.

'No! Wait!' shouted Steve.

He had them.

They stopped.

'His name is Mr Guess.'

'Poor guy,' said Charlie.

'It could be worse: his name could be Charlie Guess.' Tim couldn't resist it and Charlie tried hard not to smile. There they were, laughing like maniacs about absolutely nothing, when they heard someone say, 'Well, what have we here?'

It was big Charlie, surrounded by his friends. 'I think it's the new dweeb,' laughed one of big Charlie's friends.

Charlie was beginning to get angry. 'Takes one to know one,' he retorted.

'Oh, it's got a tongue,' laughed one of the big kids.

Just then someone came their way, calling, 'Leave off, you lot.'

Everyone turned. Steve groaned – it was Terri, his sister.

'Hi, Terri, what's the matter with you?' said big Charlie.

'That's my brother and his friends – don't give them a hard time.'

'Sure thing, Terri,' replied another of big Charlie's group. 'We didn't know.'

Big Charlie came over to Charlie, hand out-stretched. 'Sorry, mate, only having a bit of fun – no hard feelings.'

Charlie had the grace to shake his hand. 'Yeah, OK,' he mumbled.

'What's your name?' asked the older boy.

'Charlie.'

They all laughed. 'I suppose that means I'm your godfather. You have any problems, just let me know.'

Big Charlie turned to Terri. 'All right?'

Terri smiled. 'Thanks, Charlie.'

Steve grimaced. Why did she always have to save him? Then he noticed the way his sister and big Charlie smiled at each other.

Oh, no, he thought, *not another boyfriend*. He couldn't stand it when his sister was in love – he could never get near the telephone.

CHAPTER FIVE

Marilyn's Terror

'What do you think you're looking at, fish-face?'

The girl froze, startled by the voice.

'You. I'm talking to you.'

Marilyn looked in the direction of the voice. It belonged to a big girl with funny hair and an ugly sneer.

She didn't know what to say. 'Me?'

'Me, me,' mimicked the girl. 'Yes you, monkey's breath.'

Marilyn felt her face flushing. 'I wasn't looking at you,' she said, trying to appear nonchalant. But her own voice sounded high and shaky. The older girl went in for the kill.

'Come 'ere, you.'

Marilyn looked around, hoping that someone else would come into the toilets, where she now found herself trapped. Why was this girl picking on her? She didn't even know her. It was only her first day at the new school.

No one came. Marilyn began to feel frightened.

'I said, come 'ere.'

Marilyn walked over to the girl.

'What's your name?'

'M-M-M-M-M-Marilyn,' she stuttered. Tears

came to her eyes as she heard herself. She had tried so hard not to stammer and had vowed never to do it at the new school. Now, she felt humiliated.

'I guess you're a baby – you cry and you can't talk.' The big girl laughed. Marilyn just stood there with her head down. 'Now listen, baby M-M-M-Marilyn, in this school, the new kids do what the older ones say, right?'

Marilyn didn't move.

'*I said, right?*'

Marilyn nodded.

'Not good enough, toad, say "Yes, Miss".'

Marilyn tried, but could not get the words out. The older girl laughed again.

'One or two other little rules you need to know. It costs money to use these toilets and I'm the person you pay – for using the loos, using the water and using the towel. It adds up, you know. But since you're new, I'll give you a special bargain . . .'

Marilyn could hardly hear the girl, her heart was pounding so loudly.

'Let's say you only use the toilets once a day, five days a week. I won't charge you for Saturday or Sunday, being the generous sort. That means you pay me once a week until further notice. I'll take the first instalment now.' She held out her hand expectantly.

Marilyn gulped. She only had a little money with her and that was supposed to be her bus fare, until she got a pass. She shook her head.

The girl suddenly turned very nasty. She grabbed the front of Marilyn's jumper and glared into her face. 'Hand it over or I'll thump you, toad!'

Marilyn reached into her new bag, but the girl was too quick for her. She grabbed the bag, turned it upside-down and scooped up the change off the floor.

'Meet me here tomorrow for the next instalment and, baby M-M-Marilyn, not a word to anyone or the price goes up, double, understand?'

Marilyn nodded again and bent down to collect the rest of her things. She was really crying now. *What have I ever done to that girl?* she thought. *Nothing*. It wasn't fair.

Marilyn locked herself into a cubicle and sat on top of the toilet seat. She couldn't go to class crying. You didn't do that in secondary school. She wished she had a friend, any friend. She didn't know anyone yet and now no one would want to know her if they saw her looking like this. It was almost time to go to class. She heard someone outside. Not daring to come out in case it was the bully again, Marilyn stood quietly on the seat and peered out over the top.

It was there that Gill and Amy found her, just a bit of her hair and two big brown eyes over the top of the loo door.

'What on earth you doing up there?' said Amy.

'Is anyone e-e-else th-there?'

'No one here but us,' answered Gill.

Marilyn got down, unlocked the door and looked out, carefully surveying the place.

'What's the matter?' said Gill, combing her hair.

Marilyn just shrugged. 'N-n-nothing.'

Gill and Amy looked at her. Marilyn felt incredibly shy. How she wanted to tell them. Instead, she tried to smile and went over to one of the wash basins, as far away from the girls as she could get.

Gill started talking to Amy. 'I think that Terri likes Charlie, don't you?'

'What!' exclaimed Amy.

Gill gave her a withering look. 'Not our Charlie, silly, big Charlie.'

They both giggled.

'Do you think I should start wearing lipstick?' asked Gill.

'Yeah,' said Amy. 'You're kind of pale.'

Gill stared hard into the mirror. Amy was right – she looked like a ghost with flaming red hair. She hated having red hair – why couldn't it be blonde or brown or any other colour? Gill sighed and turned away.

Marilyn still said nothing, just washed her face and dabbed at her eyes. Listening to the two girls talk, she felt a pang of loneliness.

'You sure you don't want to tell us what happened?' Gill was trying to be kind, but this girl just wouldn't respond.

Marilyn started to take a deep breath. Maybe they could help her . . .

Just then, the bell rang. Gill looked at her, giving her one more chance, but Marilyn had lost her nerve. She shook her head again.

'OK,' said Gill. 'See you later.' Gill and Amy hurried towards class. Marilyn followed behind, slowly, cautiously looking for the bully. She was beginning to dread the school year she had so looked forward to last summer.

Gill and Amy walked quickly, talking about

nothing, but enjoying it. The rest of the girls came from the playground, followed by Charlie and the boys. Gill turned a critical eye on Charlie. He was laughing and joking, his face alive with fun. *He's cute*, thought Gill, *sometimes*.

Then she felt embarrassed. What would the girls think if she told them Charlie was cute? Probably laugh her out of school. When they got to the door of the classroom, they raced in to find a table.

'Hey, Gill,' called Julia, 'over here.' She had one table, the boys another.

From what she'd heard, she decided that she was going to like this teacher. Someone had said he had a sense of humour. Even if he didn't, all her friends were here. Couldn't be all bad!

CHAPTER SIX

Guess

Mr Guess was the tallest teacher they had ever had. In fact, he was one of the tallest men they had ever *seen*. He would have been quite frightening, if he hadn't smiled so much. Steve's sister said most of the kids really liked him. He wrote on the blackboard:

1. 2 metres
2. Guess – NOT a joke
3. Basketball
4. 45 years ancient
5. Wife, plus two
6. Boys

Underneath he wrote:

The most commonly asked questions –
here are the answers

Mr Guess introduced himself properly and then told them what had happened to him the day before when he had been waiting in a queue at the shop. A man had hurried past everyone and tried to cut in. He had stepped in front of the man standing in front of Mr Guess. Mr Guess did not know either of them.

The man in front of Mr Guess was about 1.6 metres tall. He had poked his umbrella into the back of the queue-jumper. 'Excuse me,' the man had said. 'There's a queue here.'

The queue-jumper had looked at the short man and snorted. 'You gonna fight me about it?'

'No,' answered the man. Then he had turned to a startled Mr Guess and said, 'But he is.'

Mr Guess had put on his fiercest frown. The queue-jumper had looked up at him and quietly walked to the back of the queue.

The class laughed. 'Good for you,' said Charlie. He wished Mr Guess had been in the park when the bullies had attacked him. He could hear himself now as the bully had said, 'What are you going to do about it?' 'Nothing,' replied Charlie, 'but *he* is.' Imagine their surprise as they turned around, looked up and up and up at Mr Guess. *Now that would be real justice*, he thought.

Mr Guess was continuing: 'The irony,' he said, 'is that I never get into fights and I was glad that my size and frown were enough to end it. When I was in school, I always seemed to get into trouble because I was big. I was actually quite timid, but if there was any disturbance and I was anywhere near it, the teachers automatically assumed that I was the bully.'

At the mention of the word 'bully', Gill's ears perked up. *I wonder if he's heard about what happened to Charlie and me? Probably not*, she thought.

Just then, the door to the classroom opened and the girl Gill and Amy had seen in the toilets tried to come in quietly. Unfortunately, she managed to drop her books, her bag and her lunch box just as she got to her seat. Everyone stared. The girl turned scarlet and mumbled something that sounded like 's-s-sorry'.

Mr Guess stopped, and said kindly, 'Never mind, come in.' Then he carried on as if nothing had happened. Marilyn refused to look up, but was relieved that he didn't shout. If anyone shouted at her, she would burst into tears.

Gill whispered to Amy, 'That's the girl we just talked to before class.'

'I wonder who she is?' replied Amy.

Mr Guess cleared his throat. 'As I was saying, I was labelled a bully, but never was one. Has that ever happened to anyone here?' They looked around at each other, too embarrassed to respond.

Mr Guess was silent for a minute or so, to give them a chance to speak. No one did.

'Right,' he said. 'You know this class is about Personal and Social Education and that we are going to discuss various issues which are important to you, such as personal safety, bullying, sex education' – giggles – 'and relationships. I understand that many of you have already had the Kidscape safety programme in school. Can anyone remember some of the things you learned?' No one moved. 'Speak to me,' joked Mr Guess. 'I won't bully you, I promise.'

At the mention of bullies, Katie raised her hand. 'If someone bullies you, you should get friends to help.'

Mr Guess wrote that on the board. 'Anything else?' he prompted.

Charlie, Gill and Julia stuck up their hands.

'Shout NO and run away.'

'Tell someone.'

'Stay with a group.'

Marilyn peeked at the board. She didn't know any of this. In her school they had only had lessons, not discussions about bullies. Besides, she didn't have a group of friends here to help her and she certainly couldn't shout NO to anyone.

Mr Guess finished writing and turned to them. 'One of the most common problems that kids tell me about is bullying. I spent part of the summer in Norway and they call it "mobbing" there. But in Norway they have done something about mobbing. They have class rules, class meetings to discuss problems and the students put on role-plays about it. You've probably all done some role-plays before, but has anyone come from a school that had class rules?'

One or two hands went up.

'What do you think of the idea?'

Gill was beginning to think that Mr Guess didn't know about the bullies that she and Charlie had encountered. This seemed to be just one of the things he talked about. She felt a bit more comfortable. At first she had thought he was trying to get them to tell about something he already knew about. Grown-ups were sneaky that way.

'I think it's a good idea if the kids get to make the rules.'

'Yes,' responded Mark, 'like two-hour lunch breaks.'

'And ten-minute classes,' Tim added.

'No homework,' chimed in Deirdre.

They were getting into it now.

'All right, enough,' laughed Mr Guess. 'How about some serious rules? I would like you to meet in small groups and come up with a list of class rules you think are fair and that your parents and teachers might agree with. Try making a list of about eight or ten. Write them down and we'll discuss them.'

They looked around to see what to do. 'Go on,' said Mr Guess, a little impatiently. 'Into groups of about six. Don't just think about it, *do it*!'

Gill, Amy, Katie and Deirdre pulled their chairs around a table. They didn't know anyone else, except the boys, but they had already formed a group with a couple of other boys. Marilyn and a few others sat, not sure how to join in. 'Come on, everyone, up and move into a group somewhere. Introduce yourselves – let's go.' He walked around encouraging the children to sit at tables. Marilyn moved towards Gill's table just as two other girls sat down. Uncertain, she looked around and found another table. She quietly joined the group, thinking how awful it was not to know anyone or have any friends.

The groups were soon suggesting rules and arguing about who should write them down. The noise level rose steadily until the teacher next door stuck her head round the door and rolled her eyes. Mr Guess immediately told them to quieten down, which they did – for all of one minute. Charlie's table was the noisiest. Gill could hear Mark and Tim and Steven trying to shout one another down. Gill looked over just as Charlie glanced her way. She stuck her tongue out, he returned the favour. She didn't see Mr Guess come up to her table.

'Maybe you should add "Not Sticking Tongues Out In Class" to your rules,' he said lightly. Gill blushed to the roots of her hair – her face *was* the colour of her hair. Charlie grinned and ducked his head.

They were so engrossed in talking and getting the rules written that no one realized that the class was almost over until the bell rang.

'We'll finish this the next time we meet,' said Mr Guess as they left.

Charlie and the boys came over to Gill's table as they were clearing up. Charlie leaned over to Gill and said quietly, 'Don't you think it's strange that Mr Guess brought up bullying? Do you think he knows?'

'No,' said Gill, 'I think it's just a coincidence. Anyway, I think maybe we should tell him about those bullies. He might have some ideas.'

She wrinkled her nose – always a sign that a decision was being made. It made her look exactly like their old school gerbil, thought Charlie.

'Well, it didn't actually happen *at* school, so I think we should just get on with things and forget about it.' Charlie seemed resigned.

'Maybe we should try to find them in the park. Then we could follow them home and find out where they live.'

'Great, Sherlock,' said Charlie. 'You know we aren't supposed to go there. My mother would kill me.'

'Guess you're right,' sighed Gill, uncertain about what to do.

Most of the kids had now left the room, hurrying

to get to their other classes. Gill and Charlie didn't notice the time. Mr Guess came up at that moment to shoo them out. They walked off, still deep in conversation.

Term had begun . . .

CHAPTER SEVEN

The Bullies Come Back

The school year was flying by. Autumn had been fairly mild, but now winter had descended with a vengeance. *Maybe we'll have snow for Christmas*, thought Gill, as she pulled up her scarf to keep her face warm. Christmas was her favourite holiday of the year. Already the house smelled festive, with brandy puddings, cakes, biscuits and the pine tree standing outside the door in a bucket of water. They would put it up this weekend and decorate it.

Gill's job was to dig the boxes out of the attic. She loved unwrapping those magical glass bulbs and lights, and all the ornaments they had made over the years. Grandma and Grandpa would be there, talking about the old days with Gill half listening, half watching the patterns the tree made on the ceiling. She didn't think she would ever get tired of Christmas, even if she lived to be 103, like her great-grandmother. No one at school had believed her until she'd brought in the newspaper clipping. Imagine living that long – 103 Christmasses! Lucky old thing. When she was young, they used to put real candles on the trees. So had her mother. Her grandmother told her that during the war, they couldn't afford to have trees, so they would just light candles and pretend. They had saved up all their ration cards for a chicken and some sugar.

Gill sighed. How could anyone live in a world without sugar?

She was so lost in thought that at first she didn't notice Charlie fall into step beside her. They walked to school together most days. They talked about the holidays and how glad they were for a break from homework. Homework was like a bad tooth pain – no matter what you did you couldn't get away from it. The only person who didn't load them down was Mr Guess and that was because they discussed things so much. Hard to have a discussion for homework. Gill and Charlie were laughing when they reached the gates. 'Only six more days to go,' chanted Charlie as they turned into the school.

'Only six more days to go,' someone said sarcastically. 'Ain't they a cute couple?'

'If it isn't little Miss Red and her friend Spotted Dick.'

'Look, Liz, they go to our school. How nice.' Brian came right up to them. 'Move, worms.'

Gill and Charlie gulped.

'You can't scare us,' said Gill, looking daggers at Liz. Her teeth were chattering from the cold . . . and a bit from fright.

'Brave little worms, ain't ya?' sneered Al.

'Where've you been hiding?' said Liz, menacingly.

'Never came back to see us, did you?' contributed Digger.

'Yeah, we waited and waited. Perhaps you don't like us?' said Al.

'And we're so likeable, aren't we?' Liz laughed.

'I think you're about to have another accident, creep.' Brian looked straight at Charlie.

Moving behind Charlie, Brian put out his foot. Al casually walked over and brushed against him, forcing Charlie to trip on to the tarmac.

It happened so quickly that Gill didn't have time to react. The playground was almost deserted – too cold for anyone to stand around watching. Anyway, if they had seen it it would have looked as though Charlie had fallen over accidentally.

Gill stared hard at Liz. 'You're really big when it comes to picking on younger kids, aren't you?'

'Oh, it's got a nasty mouth on it.'

Liz wasn't filled with the Christmas spirit, obviously. Gill looked around at a few people in the distance hurrying into the building. No help there. They were bent almost to the ground against the wind, anyway.

'Look,' said Gill in her most reasonable tone, 'we've never done anything to you. Let's just leave it.'

Liz glared. 'You are in *my* school and that offends me.'

Just then the morning bell went off and one of the teachers ran by, trying to make his class on time. 'Come on, you lot, we're all late,' he shouted as he rushed past. Gill and Charlie, now on his feet, seized this remark and tore after him. They didn't stop running until they reached their first class, Music.

Puffing to catch their breath, they joined in the carols and chanaka songs that they were going to present at the assembly next week. Gill sang dutifully, but her mind was thinking how she hated the bullies for ruining her holiday mood.

'Tomorrow, don't be here,' Liz had yelled after them, in a menacing voice. 'And don't tell anyone, either, or you'll be sorry.'

What bad fortune has made Liz a pupil at our school? thought Gill. *Why haven't we seen her until now? Too many kids here, I suppose.* With over a thousand pupils it wasn't that odd that they hadn't met before. Still, Gill was furious. Everything had been going so well.

Charlie was having trouble concentrating on the words to the songs. He felt like a mouse in the grip of a boa constrictor. He heard the refrain from the nursery-school song going through his head. Instead of 'We Wish You A Merry Christmas', he was singing:

I'm being swallowed by a Boa Constrictor
I'm being swallowed by a Boa Constrictor
I'm being swallowed by a Boa Constrictor
And I don't like it much.

Oh, no! Oh, no, she swallowed my toe
Oh, gee! Oh, gee, she swallowed my knee
Oh, fiddle! Oh, fiddle, she swallowed my middle
Oh, heck! Oh, heck, she swallowed my neck
Oh, dread! Oh, dread, she swallowed my he . . .

It went round and round in his head, no matter what song the teacher, Ms Carter, chose. He hardly heard a word she said, worrying about what might happen after school. What if they were waiting for him?

The lesson over, Gill and Charlie agreed to meet later and tell the others. Maybe they could go over to Gill's and decide what to do.

CHAPTER EIGHT

What To Do

School was out. Charlie wasn't sure if he should be thrilled or terrified. When he walked out of the school, what would he find? Would *they* be there to get him? He wished he'd gone to Tim's that day instead of sticking with Gill. This was all her fault, he thought, darkly. 'Don't be silly,' answered a little voice in his head, 'the bullies are just creeps looking for someone to pick on. Gill had nothing to do with it.'

'Hah!' replied Charlie to no one in particular.

'Hah?' said another voice, this one loud and right behind him.

Charlie jumped a mile. When he came down, Mark was standing there laughing.

'You idiot!' Charlie growled.

Mark looked offended. 'Hey! I'm on your side, remember? Come on, Charlie, don't be so touchy.'

'Sorry,' said Charlie, feeling a bit sheepish. 'Where're we meeting?'

'By the bicycle shed – let's go.'

Charlie and Mark raced over to the shed. One thing was on their side: it was absolutely freezing. The wind was so strong that running against it was like pushing into those bouncy castles they used to play on at the beach when they were little. Tiny, delicate flakes of snow were trying to come down, but the wind wouldn't co-operate with them, either. Every time they tried to land, it tossed them back up into the sky.

But Charlie couldn't complain. The bullies didn't like this weather much, either. They were nowhere to be seen.

Steve and Tim were already at the shed, stamping their feet to keep warm, hands dug deep inside their pockets.

The girls should have been here by now. Charlie was exasperated. Where *was* Gill? He hated to admit it, but he really liked seeing her. His sister (Big Bottom, BB for short) said he must love Gill. 'Gill this, Gill that – Little Brother's got a girlfriend!' she taunted him. Charlie had thrown a glass of water at her, which had missed her but hit the wall. This hadn't gone down well with his parents, who had grounded him. BB got away scot-free. There was no justice in this world. Charlie often lamented that he wasn't an only child, or that his parents had not had the foresight to have him first.

'Just you wait until I outgrow you,' he silently threatened his sister. That would be soon, if he continued to grow as he had recently. BB only had a couple of centimetres on him now. 'Just you wait, you old BB, just you wait!' Charlie knew all the words to the musicals. His dad played them all the time. Charlie loved all kinds of music and had a good singing voice. He wasn't even embarrassed to sing in front of his friends. Actually, Charlie liked acting, as well, and had even managed to get a part in the school play, much to the delight of his parents.

'Where the heck are they?' he said aloud.

'There they are,' said Tim, pointing.

He saw them in the distance. Deirdre, Gill, Katie, Amy and Julia came hurrying, the wind catching their hair and clothes. Even so they were chattering away and laughing loudly.

How can they laugh with all this going on? thought Charlie, a bit dramatically.

'Come on,' shouted Gill. 'Let's go to my house.' She waved her arm in a vast circle. *Gill wouldn't be able to talk if you held her hands still*, thought Charlie. Then he blushed, thinking of holding her hand.

The boys ran over to join them and they all headed for Gill's. Her mum never minded how many kids were in the house. She always found something for them to eat and left them alone. Most of them envied Gill her mum. But her little sister, Anne, was something else. Noisy and nosey, you just could not get rid of her. Maybe Anne would be having a nap.

No such luck. When they walked in the door, Anne toddled over and put her hands into the air. 'Pick up!' she demanded of Tim, who scooped her up and gave her a hug. Tim was used to kids. He had twin brothers and a sister. His sister was in a wheelchair and Tim often took her on outings to the park.

Anne drooled on Tim's face, which was too much even for him. He quickly put her down.

'Ugh!' chorused Charlie and Steve. 'Yuck!'

Tim shrugged and went to wash it off.

'I'm not having children, ever,' said Amy. She planned to become a doctor and wouldn't have time, anyway, she reasoned.

'Me neither,' replied Mark.

Steve, who had sworn himself to bachelorhood, now added remaining childless to his vow.

Gill's mum laughed. 'None of you ever drooled, I suppose?'

Charlie had picked up Anne and was feeding her a biscuit from the table. He wished he could swap his older sister for a younger one. Much more fun than BB. He grinned, thinking how much she hated his nickname for her. *Genius, Charlie, pure genius*, he thought, modestly.

'Help yourself to drinks and biscuits,' said Gill's mum, as she left the room.

A second invitation wasn't necessary. The walk and the cold had made them ravenous.

'Wait a minute, Mum,' asked Gill. Her mother stopped and turned. 'You remember those bullies at the end of last summer?'

'Yes.'

'Well, they go to our school.'

'Oh, dear,' sighed Gill's mum. 'When did you find that out?'

They told her what had happened, each one eager to supply more details.

She listened until they had finished.

'Did you tell the Headteacher?'

'No,' replied Charlie.

'We hardly know her,' Gill added.

'I think we should ring her now and tell her what happened.'

The children were silent, not sure what to do.

'Maybe she'll think we're a bunch of babies who can't take care of ourselves,' said Julia.

'This gang also mugged Katie in the park – they are probably well known to the school.'

'It's not fair that they get away with it,' said Gill.

'True,' replied Charlie, 'but they'll be furious that we turned them in. They'll probably wait and get us when no one's around.'

'But remember what we talked about in Mr Guess's class?' said Amy. 'Bullying shouldn't be allowed.'

'Maybe we should bring it up at the class meeting,' suggested Deirdre.

'That's a good idea,' agreed Julia.

'Who is going to talk first?' asked Tim. He was shy talking in front of a group. He knew he didn't want to be the first.

'I don't mind,' said Amy. 'I'll start and then you join in.'

'OK.' Gill didn't mind, she wasn't shy. 'Mr Guess is nice – he'll listen. He's like Mrs Simpson,' she sighed. 'I really liked her.'

'*She* said you should always tell if someone bullied you.'

Mrs Simpson had been their teacher two years ago – one of their all-time favourite teachers. She taught them about saying no, getting friends together and telling if someone bullied you.

'That was at the primary school. We're in secondary school now. Things are different,' Mark objected.

Katie shook her head. 'Uh-uh – bullies are still bullies.'

'Except they're bigger and meaner,' said Charlie.

They were silent again.

'By the way, how's Mrs Simpson's little girl?' Julia asked Gill's mum.

'Walking and talking and causing havoc!'

'Doesn't seem possible that she's nearly two.'

'Maybe we should go over to see her,' said Deirdre.

'Good idea,' agreed Tim. 'Then she could drool on me – join the club!'

'Mrs Simpson doesn't drool, you wally,' Julia retorted.

They laughed. But the problem of the bullies was still at hand. What should they do?

'Maybe we should also call the police and tell them we can identify them now,' said Gill.

'But that was months ago and the police said we needed more proof – like witnesses or the other victims to come forward. Otherwise we couldn't take it to court.' Charlie frowned. 'Besides, what happened today was just a little "accident".'

Gill agreed reluctantly. 'You're right – again no witnesses – it's their word against ours. Anyway, they're bound to say it was an accident.'

'Or that they didn't even talk to us!' exclaimed Charlie.

'I think we should all stick together and not let them get any of us alone. We'll walk to school together, meet in the playground together and shout at them if they try anything.' Katie was definite.

'Remember the yell we learned – deep and loud,' said Julia.

'Aaaaaagh!' yelled Deirdre suddenly. Everyone jumped. Anne thought it was funny. She rushed over to Deirdre and said, 'Pick up.'

'Not on your life, kiddo.' Deirdre didn't want drool in her plaits. Anne screwed up her face and started sniffling.

'All right, just this once, but don't you slobber on me, you little monkey.' Deirdre held her as much at arm's length as she could. Anne pulled Deirdre's hair and tried to chew it on the ends. Deirdre grimaced, but bravely kept holding her.

Gill's mother listened until they stopped talking. 'It all sounds good, but I think telling Mr Guess at school is really important. Charlie, you need to tell your parents, as well.'

'OK,' said Charlie. 'I guess we better do something or they'll bother us for the rest of our lives.'

'So we'll tell Mr Guess tomorrow at class meeting,' offered Amy.

'All right,' said Gill.

'We'll all back you up,' said Tim. 'After all, what are friends for – right, Charlie?'

Charlie grinned and breathed a sigh of relief. Now that they had a plan, he felt ten times better.

CHAPTER NINE

Telling

'Only five more days of class, in case you hadn't noticed.' Mr Guess was clearly as delighted to have a holiday as they were. 'Today we'll start with the class meeting.'

The class meeting was held once a week to discuss problems or things that were bothering people, or to tell about a classmate's achievements. It was a good chance to clear the air. They all pulled their chairs into a circle and waited. Mr Guess started. 'There are one or two people I'd like to say something to. Tim, I understand that you have won a science competition being run by the National Young Scientists Association. Would you like to tell us a bit about it?'

Tim felt himself flush, though he was secretly quite pleased. He never would have mentioned it. The others listened as he explained his project and there were gasps as he told them the prize – a trip to the Kennedy Space Centre in Florida and, of course, a side-trip to Disney World and Epcot.

'Mrs Briggs will make a special announcement about this to the whole school in assembly, but I wanted to congratulate you here,' concluded Mr Guess.

'Wow!' enthused Mark. 'Wish I'd paid more attention to science.'

'Nice going, Tim,' said Charlie.

The group burst into spontaneous applause, something that rarely happened in class meetings.

Tim beamed and tried, not very successfully, to look modest.

Mr Guess spoke again. 'The other matter is not as happy. Max and RJ, we've unfortunately had four more children from the primary school tell their teacher that you have been making comments when you pass them on the way home. What might they be talking about?'

Max and RJ looked decidedly uncomfortable. This wasn't the first time they'd been spoken to about this. No use lying about it; the class wouldn't believe them anyway.

Max cleared his throat. 'It was only a bit of fun, Mr Guess.'

'We didn't hit them or anything. Just made a few jokes,' added RJ.

The class looked at them. The two boys squirmed in their chairs, embarrassed by this unwanted attention.

'Well,' said Mr Guess, looking serious, 'I don't think you realize that it isn't "only a bit of fun" to the little kids. They're scared of you. What are you going to do about it?'

'Stop it,' mumbled RJ.

'Yeah,' said Max.

'Good,' replied Mr Guess, 'see that you do and I

expect you'll want to apologize to the kids, if you pass them today.'

Max and RJ nodded.

'By the way, I hope you won't give them a hard time for telling, because if you do, we shall have to carry it further. As it's nearly the holidays, I know you'll feel in a holiday mood and be kind to people, won't you?' He smiled.

Max gave a little, sick smile back and RJ just hung his head.

'Anything to add?' Mr Guess looked around the circle. No one spoke. They felt that Max and RJ had been fairly treated. Everyone knew they bugged the little children, more out of boredom than malice.

'Now,' said Mr Guess, 'who has got something they want to talk about?'

Several hands went up.

Cindy, looking woeful, told the class that her dog had been run over and killed the day before. She tried hard to control her voice, which broke as she finished her sentence. She couldn't go on. Marilyn, sitting next to her, reached over and patted her hand. It was surprising because Marilyn never spoke or joined in during the class meetings. There were tears in Marilyn's eyes. She and many of the class had pets and could sympathize over Cindy's loss, especially at this time of year.

'My dog died last year and I felt awful,' offered Sahid.

'At least he didn't feel anything – it was quick,' said Amy.

'My rabbits got a disease and both of them died

on the same day – it was terrible. I'm really sorry about your dog,' said Julia. She was very tender-hearted and loved animals.

Cindy sniffed. 'Thanks,' she said quietly.

'I'm sorry that happened, Cindy. It isn't easy to have a pet die, especially so suddenly. We can talk about it during lunch, if you like.' Mr Guess looked around the room and called on George.

George was worried about the amount of homework they were being given. The others nodded vigorously. 'Last night I had three hours of homework, all of it due today.'

'Was any of it assigned a while ago and you just waited until the last minute?' questioned Mr Guess.

'Only one thing, and that took about half an hour. The other two and a half hours were all assigned yesterday.'

Other hands went up, eager to talk. All had similar tales.

'Last Wednesday, five teachers gave me assignments. It took me nearly four hours. I got home, had a snack, worked until dinner, ate and worked until bedtime,' said Katie emphatically 'Why don't the teachers get together and find out what they are asking us to do?'

Everyone thought that was a good idea. Mr Guess promised to bring it up at the next staff meeting.

Time was running out when Mr Guess asked if anyone else had something to add today.

Amy took a deep breath and raised her hand. 'We've got a problem with some older kids,' she began.

Mr Guess waited. 'They've been bullying a couple of kids in this class.' She looked over at Gill.

Gill then told what had happened in the playground yesterday and Charlie explained the incident in the park. Katie talked about the time Liz had taken her money.

'They told us not to tell or we'd be in big trouble,' said Charlie at the end of their story.

All this time, Marilyn was listening intently, clenching and unclenching her fists. When Mr Guess asked if anyone else had been bothered by these bullies, Marilyn desperately wanted to raise her hand, but she couldn't. How could she admit that she had been paying off Liz since school began, meeting her in the toilets every day? Even when Marilyn was sick, Liz still expected her to pay. Marilyn felt sick most of the time. She hated coming to school, knowing *she* was there, waiting for her, making fun of her, making her feel like the lowest form of life on earth. Today was the first time she knew that she wasn't the only one. That made her feel a little better. Marilyn thought she might wait until after class and then tell Mr Guess on her own. Mr Guess asked the class what they thought should happen.

'Kick them all out of school,' responded Katie, who was still annoyed about what Liz or 'Judy' had done to her. 'Or put them in a boat and push it out to sea.'

They laughed.

'Seriously, we don't have much time left. What do you suggest?' asked Mr Guess. He had noticed Marilyn's discomfort and made a note to try to talk to her privately. Maybe this would explain why she had been absent so often lately.

'I wish we had a court so we could put them on trial,' said Sahid. 'I heard about a school that did that and the bullying stopped.'

'That's a good idea,' said Tim. 'Maybe we could start one.'

Katie shook her head. 'The only problem I can see is that, being the last week of school, we need to do something right away. And there are so many things going on – assemblies, plays, choir, band. Do you think we'll have time?'

'No,' said Charlie, 'it doesn't seem realistic to try. How about having the Headteacher talk to them and their parents. Maybe that would scare them off.'

The class agreed just before the bell rang. Mr Guess said that Mrs Briggs, the Headteacher, would want to see Gill, Charlie and Katie, and maybe the others. 'No problem,' replied Charlie, sounding braver than he felt.

The others nodded.

They raced out of the door, feeling good about having it all out in the open. 'Bullies beware!' shouted Charlie, punching the air. Suddenly it wasn't just their problem any more.

'I wish we did have time for a bully court,' said Gill.

Sahid agreed. 'At the school I read about there was a boy who used to be a bully at lunch—'

Deirdre interrupted him, talking a mile a minute as they left the room. 'I heard about that – someone on the court said he shouldn't be allowed to eat at all during the day – would make him too weak to bully!' They hooted so loudly that the laughter echoed back at them from down the hall. This only made it worse and soon they were convulsed with loud, snorting giggles.

Marilyn watched them go. She took her time leaving, carefully gathering her books and papers. Mr Guess walked over to her, hoping she might talk to him. Smiling gently, he said, 'You know, Marilyn, I've been a bit worried about you. Is there anything you'd like to talk about?'

Marilyn hesitated. She liked Mr Guess. Maybe she *should* tell him. Then she remembered Liz's snarling face. 'Oh, I'm OK, Mr Guess,' she said, keeping her face down so he couldn't tell she was frightened to talk. 'I've got to hurry – see you!'

Mr Guess watched her go. He knew something was wrong, but there was nothing more he could do until Marilyn asked for his help.

Marilyn turned and gave him a wave. Walking away, she thought, *If only I could be as brave as Gill.*

CHAPTER TEN

Marilyn Makes Friends

As soon as they caught their breath, they talked about telling on the bullies. They felt glad it was over.

'It wasn't so bad!' exclaimed Tim, walking towards the lockers.

'No,' said Charlie. 'I think we did the right thing.' At the back of his mind he was still a bit worried, but he didn't let it show. Would the bullies get him when they found out he'd told? The boa constrictor rhyme started again, but he firmly turned it off. 'Enough,' he said under his breath.

'What?' asked Gill, catching up with him.

'Oh, nothing,' he replied quickly. 'Nothing at all.'

'Have you done your Maths homework?' Gill wanted to know.

'Yes, have you?'

'I have, but I can't say I really understand it.'

Deirdre and Julia were still whooping over the story of the lunchtime bully as they turned down the hall to their class. 'See you at lunch,' said Julia as they left.

'See you.'

Charlie and Gill continued on to Maths, chatting about the class meeting and how they were both a little nervous about what would happen next. Gill was also uneasy about the test they were having in Maths the following day.

'Tell you what,' said Charlie, 'I'll come over and we can work together. Maybe it will help us both.' He laughed.

Gill smiled at him. 'Great idea. I might persuade my mum to part with a few Christmas goodies to help us think.'

They walked into class. Marilyn, following behind, wished with all her heart that Gill would see her and say hello. Maybe it would be easier to talk to her than to a teacher. Marilyn was in turmoil, wanting so badly for the bullying to end, but terrified that she would make it worse by telling.

At the end of the class, Charlie dashed off to get to PE on time. It took forever to get to the gym, change clothes and be there when Mr Hufford called the roll. He always seemed to be the last one to arrive. Today, he was determined not to be.

Gill was walking alone to English, her last class before lunch. Marilyn came up next to her and smiled shyly.

'Hi,' said Gill.

'Hi,' replied Marilyn.

'Do you understand all that Maths stuff?'

'Sort of,' Marilyn said. 'Do you?'

'Not much,' laughed Gill. 'Perhaps I'd better consider a career without algebra in it.'

'Yeah,' said Marilyn, uncertain of what to say next.

'What about you?' Gill asked.

'Oh, I don't know, maybe I'll do something with animals. I like dogs and cats.'

'Have you got a pet?' asked Gill wistfully. Her parents had always told her that pets were too much trouble. Her mum didn't want to get stuck taking out the dog when she wasn't there. As much as Gill protested that she would take care of it, no matter what, it was to no avail. It was the one thing she felt her parents weren't fair about. *Everyone* else had a pet.

'I've got a dog and two cats,' replied Marilyn.

'Lucky you!' Gill was envious.

Marilyn reached her class first. She turned to Gill and said lightly, 'See you!'

'See you tomorrow. Don't study too much for the test – so we can all flunk it together!' Then Gill was off.

Marilyn felt glowy inside. Gill had been so nice to her. She found a seat in her class. Maybe she'd invite her over to see her pets. That would be a good way to make friends. 'Lucky you,' Gill had said. *If only she knew how unlucky I am*, thought Marilyn. Then she brightened again, remembering their conversation. She was actually smiling to herself when the teacher came in.

'You seem cheerful today,' said Mrs Fry as she passed by Marilyn's desk. She was pleased to see Marilyn looking happy for a change. Usually she sat in class like a frightened rabbit, always getting her work in, but never opening her mouth or even hinting that she enjoyed anything.

Marilyn looked up and smiled. Maybe life wasn't so bad, after all. Now, if she could just tell someone about the bullying, perhaps she could start feeling happy again. She resolved to try.

Down the hall, Gill sat half listening to Ms Barry. English was one of her best subjects and Ms Barry always kept her attention. Not today. Even the jokes flew over Gill's head. She expected the door to open any minute and for Mrs Briggs to beckon for her to follow. She saw the bullies standing there, ready to pounce because she'd told. 'We told you not to tell, now your kid sister gets it,' snarled Liz. Gill stared, horrified, as they tossed Anne around like a rag doll. She was screaming and appealing to Gill to help her, but Brian pinned her arms firmly at her sides. 'Leave her alone, you Gargantuan Gargoyles!' exploded Gill. Digging her elbows into Brian's ribs, she hurled herself at Liz, knocking her to the ground. Grabbing Anne, she charged out the door and . . .

'Gill?' Ms Barry said for the third time.

'What? . . . Excuse me, Ms Barry, I wasn't listening.' She heard giggles around her.

'I asked you to explain the difference between an adjective and an adverb.'

Gill recovered enough to answer. She forced herself to pay attention for the rest of the lesson. When the bell signalled the end of class, she shot out of the room like an escaped convict. Dropping her books in her locker, Gill headed for the toilets so she could comb her hair before lunch.

She gave the door a shove and heard a dull thud on the other side. Marilyn emerged, looking slightly dazed. Gill was instantly apologetic. 'Are you all right? Sorry, I was just rushing and didn't think.'

'I'm fine,' said Marilyn. Gill didn't seem convinced. 'No, really, I'm OK, thanks.'

'Where you going?' Gill asked.

'Lunch,' said Marilyn. She hated lunch. She brought hers so that she could sneak away somewhere on her own and eat it. Better than not having anyone to sit with.

'Me, too,' said Gill. 'Why don't you sit with us? Then you can tell me about your dog.'

Marilyn couldn't believe it. She scarcely dared talk in case she woke up and found it was a dream.

'G-great,' she managed to say before Gill pulled her down the hall towards the canteen.

The rest of the kids made room at the table for Marilyn and Gill plyed her with questions about her dog Duchess, and Oscar and Esmeralda, her cats. Then the talk turned to the class meeting and what might happen next. Marilyn didn't say anything, just listened. After much speculation, they decamped to the playground, still including Marilyn. When the bell rang for the next lesson, Marilyn reluctantly said goodbye to her new friends and went off happily to PE.

Just as she was turning the corner, she caught sight of Liz coming towards her. But this time, Marilyn didn't meekly stop, she put on a burst of speed and ran as fast as she could right into the changing room. She peeked out to see if Liz had followed, but she hadn't – Marilyn was safe. Marilyn decided then and there that she *would* find the courage to tell about Liz. Soon.

CHAPTER ELEVEN

Justice

Mrs Briggs did not have time to deal with the bullies that day.

Marilyn managed to get home without encountering Liz. Charlie walked Gill home, where they studied for the Maths test, ate enormous amounts of Christmas goodies and talked and talked and talked. As he was leaving, Charlie squeezed her hand.

'I had fun,' he said, smiling at her. 'See you tomorrow.' Gill blushed. 'Thanks for helping with that Maths.'

'Bye.'

Charlie waved. On the way home, he thought about how easy it was to talk to Gill and how good he felt when he was with her. She was just so . . . so something. He couldn't quite put his finger on it, but whatever it was made him sing all the way home.

The next day, Mrs Briggs sent a message to Mr Guess's class, asking Charlie and Gill to come to her office during the afternoon break. In the meantime, they had the Maths test to worry about. Going into class, Gill was certain that it would be awful.

'I'm sure I'm going to fail,' she said in a worried voice to Charlie.

'That's all the faith you have in my help, huh?

Well, thanks a lot!' He grinned at her. 'Don't be silly, you'll pass – and probably get a better mark than me.'

Gill smiled in spite of herself.

'Good luck!' Charlie winked.

Charlie winking looked so comical that Gill laughed out loud. Maybe she *could* do this Maths stuff, she thought.

Mr Morton passed out the test.

Doesn't look too bad, thought Gill. As she did the test, she felt more and more confident.

At the end of class, Charlie came over. 'Well?' he questioned. 'What did you think?'

Gill crossed her fingers. 'I don't believe it, but I think I only missed a couple.'

'See, I knew you'd do OK.'

Gill saw Marilyn picking up her books. 'What did you think?' she asked.

'Not bad,' said Marilyn. 'I think he's in a good mood, so he didn't make it too hard.'

'Probably hopes we'll get him a Christmas present,' laughed Charlie, as they left.

Mr Morton was the school character. He wore outrageous wide ties, told crazy jokes and could still do a back flip from his early days as a gymnast. 'Never missed a single day in twenty-five years of teaching,' he told them. Charlie thought he was great, even if he was the Maths teacher. He planned to get him another tie for Christmas from the market, just for laughs.

The three of them chatted before heading off to their different classes.

'See you at lunch?' Gill asked Marilyn.

'Sure,' Marilyn replied.

In the canteen, they had their usual table. There were a few other kids who ate with them now. New friends they'd made since coming to the school.

Big Charlie and Terri passed by and said hello. Steve didn't mind any more. Anyway, he hardly ever saw his sister these days. She was far too busy with big Charlie.

They talked about the meeting with Mrs Briggs and what might happen. Marilyn listened, but still didn't admit that Liz was taking money from her. She felt guilty – it would help if Mrs Briggs knew about it, but she was still too frightened. In fact, she had to meet Liz after lunch today. When the kids went to the playground, Marilyn slipped away to an isolated place around the corner in the school.

'Right on time, I see. Good, hand it over.' Liz held out her hand.

Marilyn gave her the money and started to walk away.

'Not so fast, bright eyes.' Liz stopped her.

'What?' said Marilyn.

'There's an extra charge at this time of year. Christmas and all that. It's now double.' Liz's lip curled threateningly. She had this kid right where she wanted her – in her power. Liz liked the feeling.

She looked so nasty and evil that Marilyn shook. 'I-I-I don't h-h-have any m-more,' she pleaded.

'Then bring it tomorrow. Understand?' Liz glared at her. 'Or my little group of friends will have to teach you a lesson.'

Marilyn nodded miserably.

Liz walked off. Marilyn started to cry. She found

a quiet place and sat there, tears streaming down. 'It's not fair,' she thought, not for the first time. But, for the first time something else happened. Marilyn became angry. She could feel herself becoming more and more furious. *I don't deserve this*, she thought. *How dare she bully me and take my money.* The more she thought about it, the more determined she became. *I'm telling*, she decided. *Right now!*

She marched back to the playground straight to where Gill was standing with the rest of the kids. Gill looked up, startled, when Marilyn came over and said in a low voice, 'Can I talk to you?' Gill could tell that it was important. She didn't ask why, just followed her. Gill had a sixth sense about helping people. She listened carefully and didn't interrupt.

'Liz has been taking money from me every day since we started school,' said Marilyn, teeth clenched.

Gill's eyes grew wide as she listened to Marilyn's story. She wondered how many other kids Liz and her gang of bullies were bothering. When Marilyn finished, Gill put her arm around her. Marilyn felt like a ten-ton load had been lifted from her shoulders.

'I'm going to tell Mrs Briggs, too,' she said. 'That way she'll know the whole story. They won't be able to say you were making it up.' Marilyn looked defiant.

'Do you want to ask to come with Charlie and me at break?' suggested Gill. 'It might be easier to tell.'

'Let's go now,' said Marilyn. 'I'm ready.'

They went to the office and made an appointment for Marilyn to come with them that afternoon.

Later that day, Mrs Briggs talked to them all, one

at a time. She called in Katie, as well. Then she sent for Liz, Brian, Digger, Al and the others and talked to them individually. She rang parents, arranged meetings and then called them all together; bullies and victims.

They crowded into her office, no one daring to look at anyone else.

'I have just spent the entire afternoon dealing with some very unpleasant facts,' she said.

'First, there is no doubt that Liz, Al, Judy and the rest of you have been bullying and intimidating younger children – and taking money. That is completely unacceptable in this school. It's extortion and assault and I will not stand for it.' Her voice was low and firm. 'Bullies are cowards and I dislike cowardly behaviour.'

Gill and Katie looked at each other at the mention of the name Judy.

'Second, I'm sorry that I did not know about this earlier so that I could have stopped it immediately it started.' She looked at Marilyn, who was hanging her head. 'I realize that it is hard to come forward when someone has scared you to death, but remember that the policy in this school is that bullying is not tolerated. In fact, I would have hoped that you would have come to my office the minute it occurred. It would have made it easier to sort out. Remember the assembly when I talked about this being a telling school?'

Gill flushed and looked over at Charlie.

'Third, I will decide what will happen to the transgressors after I have met with their parents today. Some of you,' she said to the bullies, 'have been right

73

at the heart of this and some of you at the edges. Exactly how you were involved will determine the consequences. I expect that there will be a suspension or two.'

The bullies shifted uncomfortably.

I almost feel sorry for them, thought Gill, *but not quite*.

'Until we decide what will happen,' continued Mrs Briggs, 'I expect that you will not speak to any of these pupils or anyone else about this matter. I know,' she said, looking directly into the bullies' faces, 'that you will not say anything to any of these students *or* their friends, *or* look at them *or* gesture to them *or* write them notes. *No contact, do you understand?*' They nodded. 'And heaven help you if I find out that other things have been going on. I am going to ask that all classes have meetings tomorrow so we can uncover the full extent of your activities.'

Liz cringed.

They don't look so frightening now, thought Charlie. *Maybe Mrs Briggs is the boa constrictor*. He grinned to himself.

Marilyn snuck a glance at Liz. *She's nothing but a bully and a coward. Look at her sitting there – not so big now*, she thought.

Mrs Briggs kept the bullies in her office and allowed Gill, Charlie and Marilyn to go.

'Phew!' said Charlie. 'Boy, am I glad that's over.'

'I hope it *is*,' said Marilyn.

'But what about "Judy"?' said Gill.

'That's Digger's real name,' said Charlie. 'That's where Liz got it from when she lied to us in the park.'

'What d'you think she'll do?' asked Marilyn.

'Feed them to a boa constrictor,' laughed Charlie. Gill and Marilyn looked at him and shook their heads at each other. He had clearly gone quite demented.

CHAPTER TWELVE

Snowed In – Hurray!

It was January and it had snowed for days, closing the schools and offices. Now the snow was half a metre deep in the park and still coming down. Perfect for sledging. Gill and her friends were thrilled. No school, no homework and nothing to do but sledge, make giant snowmen (and snowwomen!), build fortresses and have massive snowball fights.

Charlie, Mark, Tim and Steve brought their sledges to the park that afternoon. There were several good hills to choose from, each covered with squealing, wet, exuberant children. They avoided the small knolls and headed for the longer runs. They expected the girls to be there and they weren't disappointed. The girls had slept over at Gill's and were already out, racing down the hills and trudging back up to the top.

Charlie could hear them as they came to the path.

'Hang on! Here we go!' Deirdre yelled as she and Julia shot downhill at high speed. Snow flew up, sending a powdery spray into their faces. Behind them came Gill and Amy together and Katie on her own. 'Ya hoo!' shouted Gill as they charged downward. 'Watch out!' screamed Katie as her sledge crashed into the others at the bottom of the hill. The five of them lay in a sodden, giggling mass. The boys looked on in amazement.

Charlie walked over and grabbed Gill's hand, helping her up. Then he helped Amy. By the time the other boys came over, the girls were dusting themselves off and ready to go again.

They all ran up the hill and positioned themselves in a line. 'The one who gets furthest down the hill wins,' declared Katie. Katie liked to make up the rules, but no one argued. It seemed fair enough to them. They let a couple of other kids go first and then set off.

'Geronimo!' yelled Charlie, as he pushed his sledge. He careered wildly down, swerving to avoid another sledge and ended up scraping past a tree completely off the path. It didn't matter as long as he kept going, bouncing over the roots before sliding to an upside-down stop. 'Not very dignified,' shouted Charlie, 'but that was some ride!'

The rest of the gang came hurtling down the slope, yelling like wild savages. The noise echoed through the trees, their branches bowing to the ground, heavy with snow. They ended up helter-skelter along the way, some making it all the way down, most falling along the trail. Amy won: she not only got to the bottom, but rolled another few metres before stopping. 'Wow!' she shouted, waving her arms in the air in victory. '*Yes!*'

They zig-zagged down about ten more times, before deciding to find some fresh, untrodden snow to make snow angels. Julia showed them how. First she found a clear, soft patch of snow and then fell backwards into it. Next, she kept her head and body still, but moved her legs back and forth, and her arms up and down. The tricky bit was getting up without ruining it. Julia had the knack, but Tim and Kate were hopeless. Their angels looked more like dragons which had fallen from great heights.

Charlie, of course, started a snowball fight. 'Wait,' shouted Katie, the organizer as usual. She soon had them divided into teams, with their territories staked out and plans of action. The battle raged for at least half an hour, by which time they were all completely covered with wet, sticky snow, frozen on to their coats, gloves and eyelashes. They were also starving and thirsty so they trudged back to Gill's, stamping their feet and blowing on their red fingers. The tip of Charlie's nose was going blue by the time they arrived.

Gill's mum poked her head around the door to see if they had all come back in one piece. Deirdre and Julia made the hot cocoa, while Tim, Steve and Amy made sandwiches. Charlie and Gill set the table, and Mark tried his best to put the drenched clothing in places where it would dry. Every radiator was steaming with gloves, scarves and macs by the time they sat down to eat. It was like sitting in a sauna, but no one complained. It felt wonderful!

'I wish we never had to go back,' sighed Mark.

'This is the life, all right,' said Charlie.

'How much longer is it supposed to last?' asked Tim.

'Two days and then a thaw's on the way from Spain or somewhere.' Steve had been following the forecasts diligently.

'Great, two more days of bliss,' said Gill. 'I just wish this had happened at Christmas.'

'Are you kidding?' Katie exclaimed. 'Then we wouldn't have time off school. Better now, just think of all the things we're missing – Maths, Science, PE, English . . .'

'The list is endless,' said Mark grinning.

'Still, a little snow at Christmas wouldn't have hurt,' Gill retorted.

'There's just no pleasing some folks,' laughed Charlie.

'There's one other thing we're missing that you didn't mention,' said Deirdre.

'What's that?' Tim asked.

'Ole Leaping Liz, the bully.'

'You know, she never said another word to us, did she?' mused Gill.

'Neither would you if you'd been suspended and threatened with the wrath of Mrs Briggs,' Steve commented.

'I almost feel sorry for her. Brian and the others never seem to be around,' said Gill.

'At least they've stopped bullying. Did you know that big Charlie had a word with them, as well?' Steve's sister had told him.

'Well, Liz still hangs around with Digger – they're a weird pair. Spiky hair and pierced noses. Yuck!' Amy shuddered.

'I heard that they've got problems at home,' said Julia.

'Yeah, but that doesn't give them the right to be bullies. Lots of people have problems at home.' Tim was not very sympathetic to bullies. He figured that if his sister in a wheelchair could cope, so could they.

'Still,' said Julia quietly, 'sometimes kids can't help what happens to them – makes them act in all sorts of strange ways.'

'Whatever the reasons, I'll never trust her. Anyway, I don't care as long as she stays away from us,' said Charlie.

'Liz hasn't bothered Marilyn, either,' Gill added. Although Marilyn wasn't one of her best friends, Gill did invite her over once in a while. Marilyn now had a circle of her own friends, but they often went to the same places. Marilyn had confided in Gill that Liz had scared her so much she had had terrible nightmares and had pretended to be sick to miss school. Actually, sometimes she didn't have to pretend, the stomach pains were so bad that they made her double over. What she had been too embarrassed to tell Gill was that she had even wet her bed a few times. She had felt she couldn't tell her mum and dad because they had enough worries. When she finally did tell them, it turned out that part of their worries was her. Anyway, that was finished and Marilyn seemed quite happy now.

'And we all got our money back,' said Charlie.

'*And* apologies,' said Gill.

'Let's forget about bullies,' pleaded Mark, 'they aren't worth wasting our breath on. Let's *do* something.'

'OK,' said Charlie in his best Humphrey Bogart voice. 'Play it, Sam, play "As time goes by".'

They all groaned. 'Did you know,' said Charlie

as they headed outdoors, 'that in *Casablanca*, Ingrid Bergman didn't say, "Play it again" – everyone always makes that mistake. She just said, "Play it".'

'Mistake, Charlie?' said Gill slyly. 'Well here's one mistake you've just made. You should have used your eyes instead of your mouth!' She pushed a handful of snow right down his back.

Believe me when I tell you that was the beginning of the all-time great snowball fight of the century.

Epilogue

Two months after that historic snowball fight, Liz and Digger were caught bullying some children from one of the primary schools. They were suspended again for three days.

In May Liz took money from and tried to bully one of the younger kids at her own school. He immediately told Mrs Briggs. The school governors decided that Liz should be expelled. She now attends a special school for children with emotional problems.

Digger is trying to remain in school and has changed her behaviour. Brian, Al and the others stopped hanging around together and are, for the most part, doing OK.

The school has posted a set of rules, which all the students, parents and staff have agreed on. The first rule is: 'Bullying of any kind – verbal, physical or emotional – is not allowed in this school.'

Appendix

Help!

If you are being bullied or know someone who is, try to get someone you know to help. If you can't or would like more advice, here are some organizations to contact:

ChildLine (0800) 1111
Kidscape (0171) 730 3300
Samaritans (0345) 909090 (local rates)
Children's Legal Centre (01206) 873820.
NSPCC (0800) 800500

Resources

Michele Elliott has written other books that deal with bullying:

For children aged 7 to 11:
The Willow Street Kids: Be Smart, Stay Safe, Macmillan, 1997

For children aged 6 and under:
Feeling Happy, Feeling Safe, Hodder Headline, 1991

For adults:
Bullying, a practical guide to coping for schools,
Longman, 1991
Keeping Safe, a practical guide to talking with children, Hodder Headline, 1988

Kidscape also has schools programmes and a free booklet entitled *Stop Bullying!* For a free copy of the booklet, send a large self-addressed envelope to:

Kidscape
152 Buckingham Palace Road
London SW1W 9TR